I0752553
SURE...I CAN SEE IT A LITTLE, I THINK.
A RESEMBLANCE.
SIGH
SICK, MAN. THANKS.
LEMME ASK YOU--

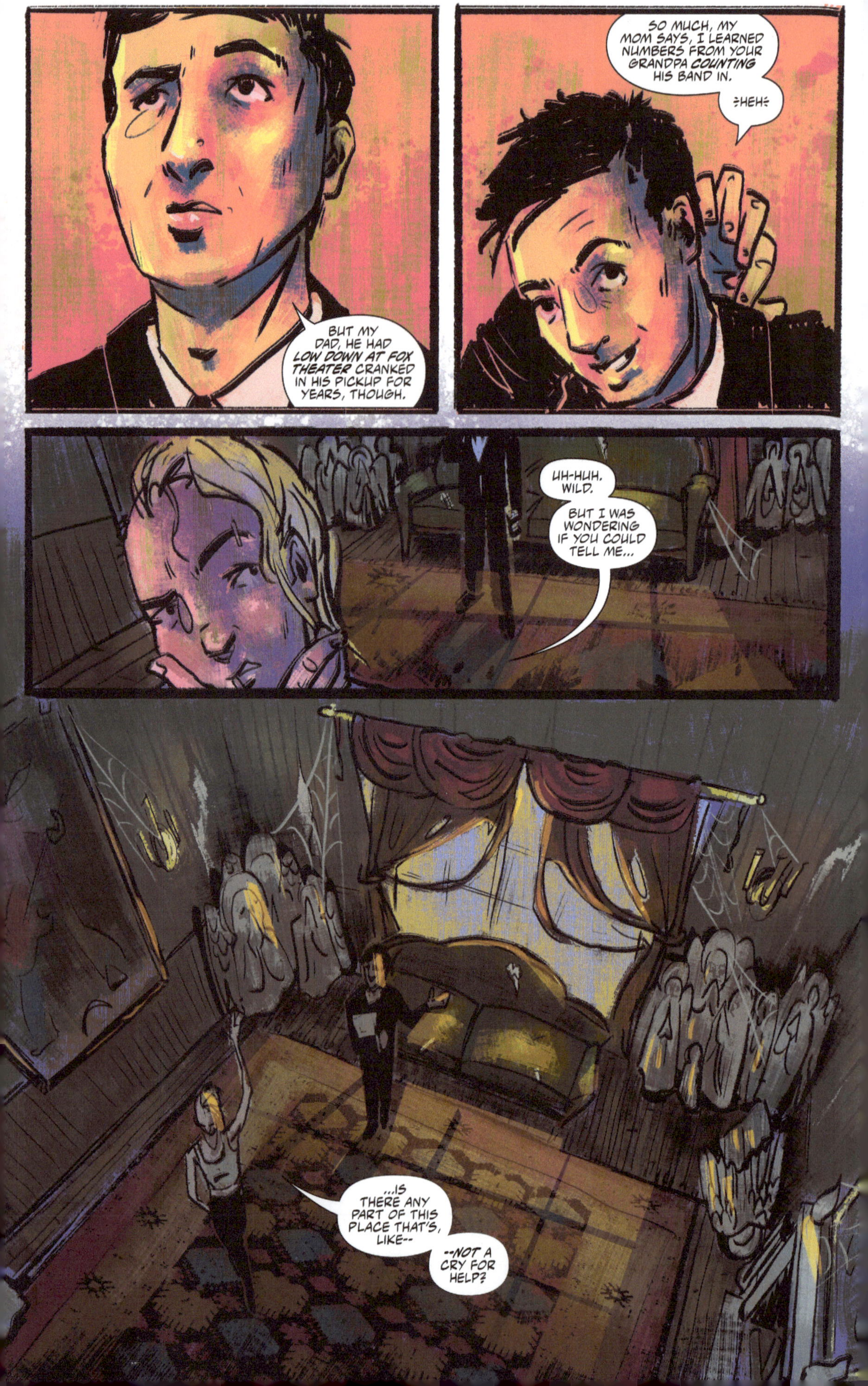

UH-HUH. WILD.

BUT I WAS WONDERING IF YOU COULD TELL ME...

...IS THERE ANY PART OF THIS PLACE THAT'S, LIKE--

--***NOT*** A CRY FOR HELP?

I MEAN, WHAT'S WITH ALL THESE GUYS?
WHY ARE THEY *INSIDE?*

CITY INSPECTORS *DID* MAKE NOTE OF THE...PECULIAR CONDITIONS.
SO YOU, UH, HAVEN'T SEEN THE PROPERTY RECENTLY? LIKE THIS?

LAST TIME I WAS HERE, I WAS *SIX,* MAYBE?
AND I NEVER REALLY KNEW HIM, SO...
...NOPE.

WELL, THE GOOD NEWS IS THE PARISH CAN'T CONDEMN THE PROPERTY UNTIL *PROBATE* ENDS.

WHOA, *"CONDEMN?"*
I JUST INHERITED THIS PLACE, LIKE, *YESTERDAY,* DUDE.

AH, ABOUT THAT... ≈AHEM≈
WE SHOULD PROBABLY TAKE A LOOK DOWNSTAIRS.

FUCKING... SHIT, MAN.
YEAH, YOU DON'T REALLY EXPECT SOMETHING LIKE THIS, DO YOU?
FROM A CELEBRITY, I MEAN.
WHAT EVEN IS ALL THIS?
A FIRE HAZARD, FOR STARTERS.
WHICH-- YOU MAY WANT TO PUT THAT CIGARETTE OUT DOWN HERE...

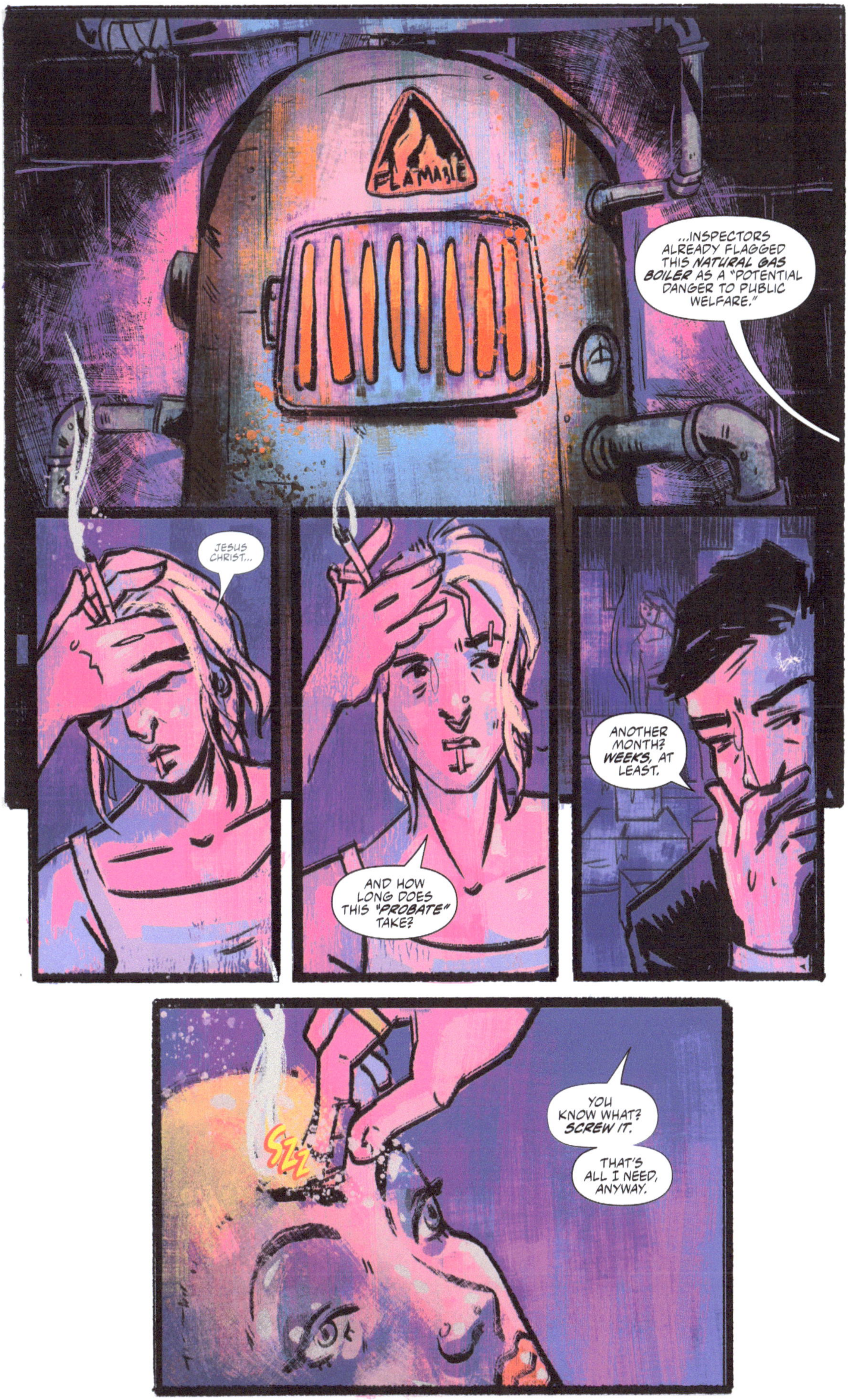

FLAMABLE

...INSPECTORS ALREADY FLAGGED THIS ***NATURAL GAS BOILER*** AS A "POTENTIAL DANGER TO PUBLIC WELFARE."

JESUS CHRIST...

AND HOW LONG DOES THIS ***"PROBATE"*** TAKE?

ANOTHER MONTH? ***WEEKS,*** AT LEAST.

TNZ: DAILY DISH
REPO BABY
--OKAY, SO THIS REPO BABY THING.
OH MY GOD...
NAPOLEONVILLE, LOUISIANA.
JUST AN HOUR OUTSIDE NEW ORLEANS.
...THE THEO VAN EVERY CRINGE CAPADES CAN'T STOP, WON'T STOP, PEOPLE!
RESEAU HOUSE
SERIOUSLY, HAS SHE BEEN OUT OF THE NEWS A SINGLE WEEK SINCE THIS BAND SIGNED WITH R&M?
I'M TELLING YOU, SHE'S GOT THIS WHOLE "INDUSTRY ROYALTY" COMPLEX...
...AND THINKS IT'S COOL TO TRASH HOTEL ROOMS LIKE IT'S 1988 OR SOMETHING
IT'S GROSS.

MAYBE SHE'S IN MOURNING. MAYBE!
WAIT-- BECAUSE HER GRAND-FATHER?!
PSSH, THAT GUY WENT OFF THE GRID IN, LIKE, THE '90S.
WELL, WE'RE BURYING THE LEDE HERE. BECAUSE THEO IS OFFICIALLY OUT OF THE BAND!
YEAH. SHE HIT A VALET WITH HER BMW IN LA LAST WEEK...
...AND THE REST OF REPO BABY FINALLY DECIDED ENOUGH'S ENOUGH.
THIS IS AFTER THE AIRPORT SECURITY THING...
AND THAT MORNING SHOW THING...
SO MANY THINGS!
AND SURPRISE, SURPRISE, THERE'S BEEN ZERO WORD FROM HER.
ALL HER SOCIALS HAVE GONE DARK SINCE THE BAND'S ANNOUNCEMENT THAT THEY'VE FIRED HER.
YESSS, GIRL! GIVE US NOTHING!
HMMMM
WHISPER-VOLT
HAHA HAHA!

WELL, WELCOME TO YOUR SOLO ERA, THEO.

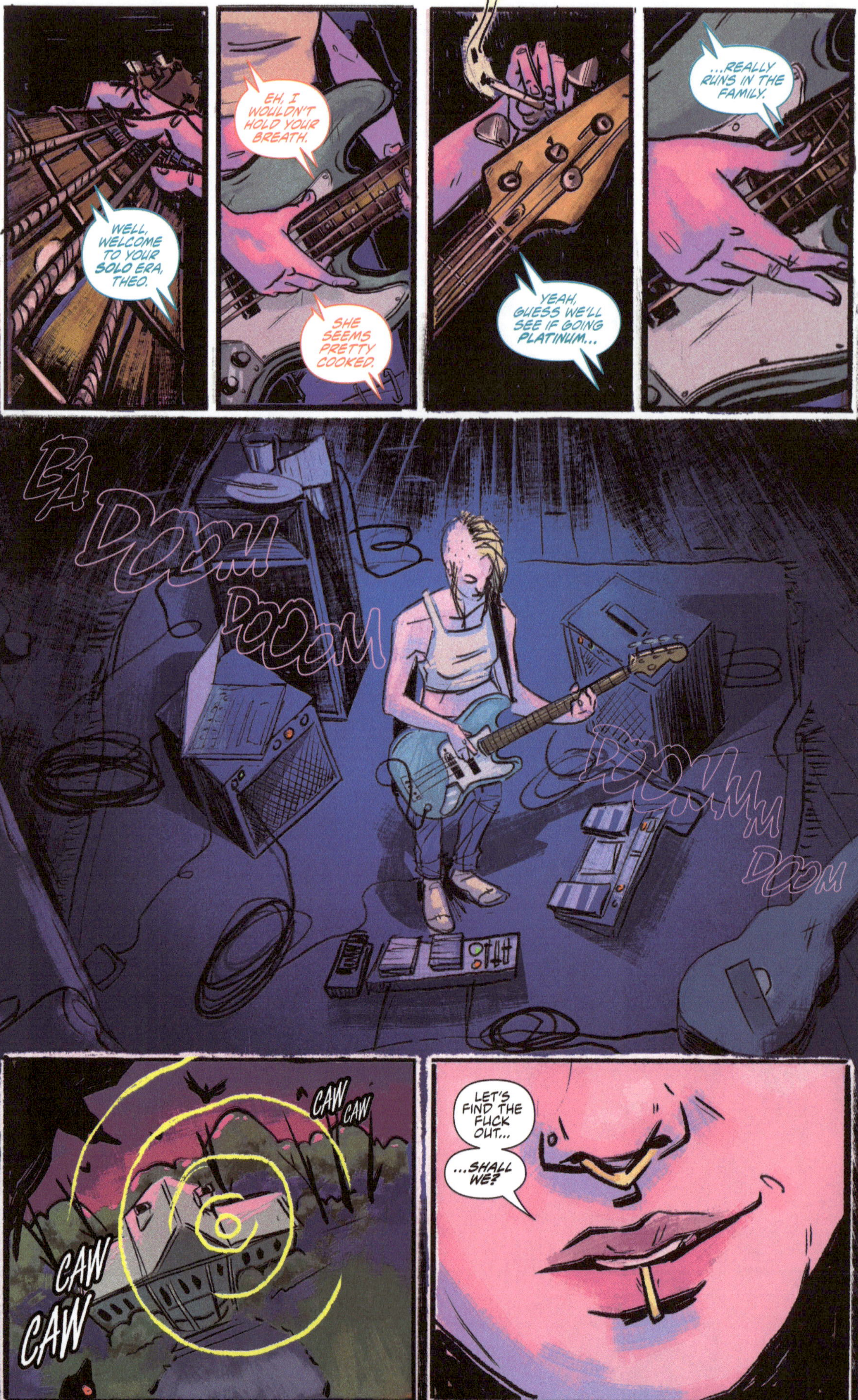

EH, I WOULDN'T HOLD YOUR BREATH.
SHE SEEMS PRETTY COOKED.

YEAH, GUESS WE'LL SEE IF GOING PLATINUM...

...REALLY RUNS IN THE FAMILY.

BA
DOOM
DOOOM
DOOMMM
DOOM

CAW
CAW
CAW
CAW

LET'S FIND THE FUCK OUT...
...SHALL WE?

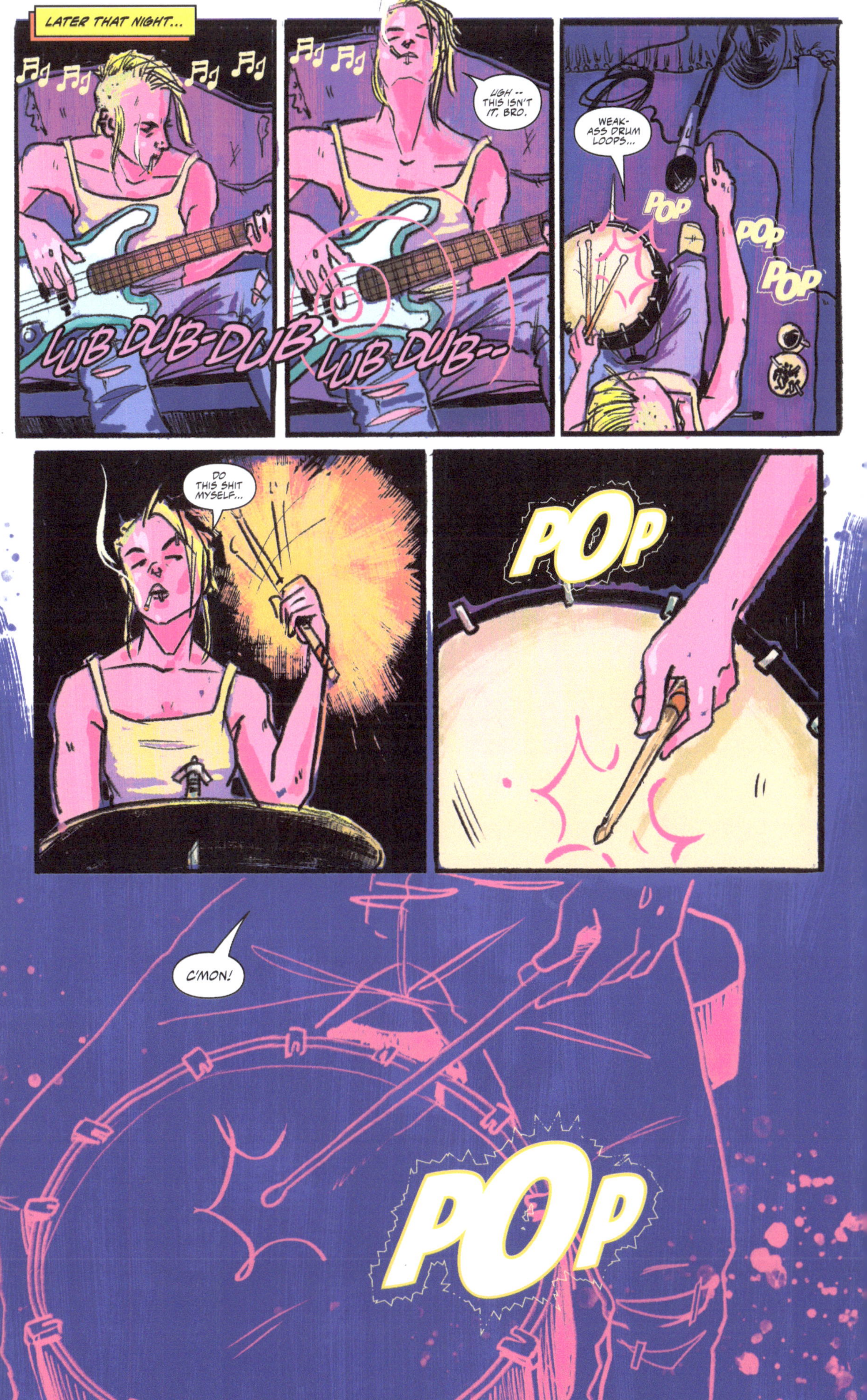
LATER THAT NIGHT...
LUB DUB-DUB
LUB DUB--
UGH -- THIS ISN'T IT, BRO.
WEAK-ASS DRUM LOOPS...
POP
POP
POP
DO THIS SHIT MYSELF...
POP
C'MON!
POP

NEEDS MORE SNAP, MAN.
⇒SIGH⇐
HMM.
KSHH
BLA
BLAM
BLAM
HERE WE GO...
CLICK
CLICK
CLICK
YESSS.
BLAMS ON DEMAND, BITCH.
TAP
TAP
TAP
BLAM
BLAM
BLAM

AND EVEN LATER STILL...
IT'S SUCH BULLSHIT!

I TOLD YOU, LAY OFF THE GOSSIP SITES FOR A WHILE.
REPO BABY DUMPS
NEPO BABY

BUT NO ONE'S HEARING MY SIDE OF IT!
THAT'S OKAY. WHAT WE'RE FIGHTING RIGHT NOW IS **OVEREXPOSURE.**

AND THE BEST RESPONSE TO ALL THIS--SIX, NINE MONTHS FROM NOW--IS GOING TO **BE BANGERS.**
SHOW PEOPLE YOU'RE CONCERNED WITH THE **MUSIC**, LIKE WE SAID.
AND HOW'S THAT GOING, BY THE WAY? WE GOT A SOLO EP YET?
I JUST ***GOT*** HERE, CHRIST.
THE PLACE IS A SHITHOLE, BUT I BROUGHT EVERYTHING I NEED TO...

...TO, UH...
HELLO?
YEAH...
...I GOTTA GO, ACTUALLY.
FINE. BUT I'M TELLING YOU, THEO, AS YOUR PUBLICIST...
...WE CAN MAKE YOU LIKEABLE AGAI--
KLIK
UM...
...HELLO?!

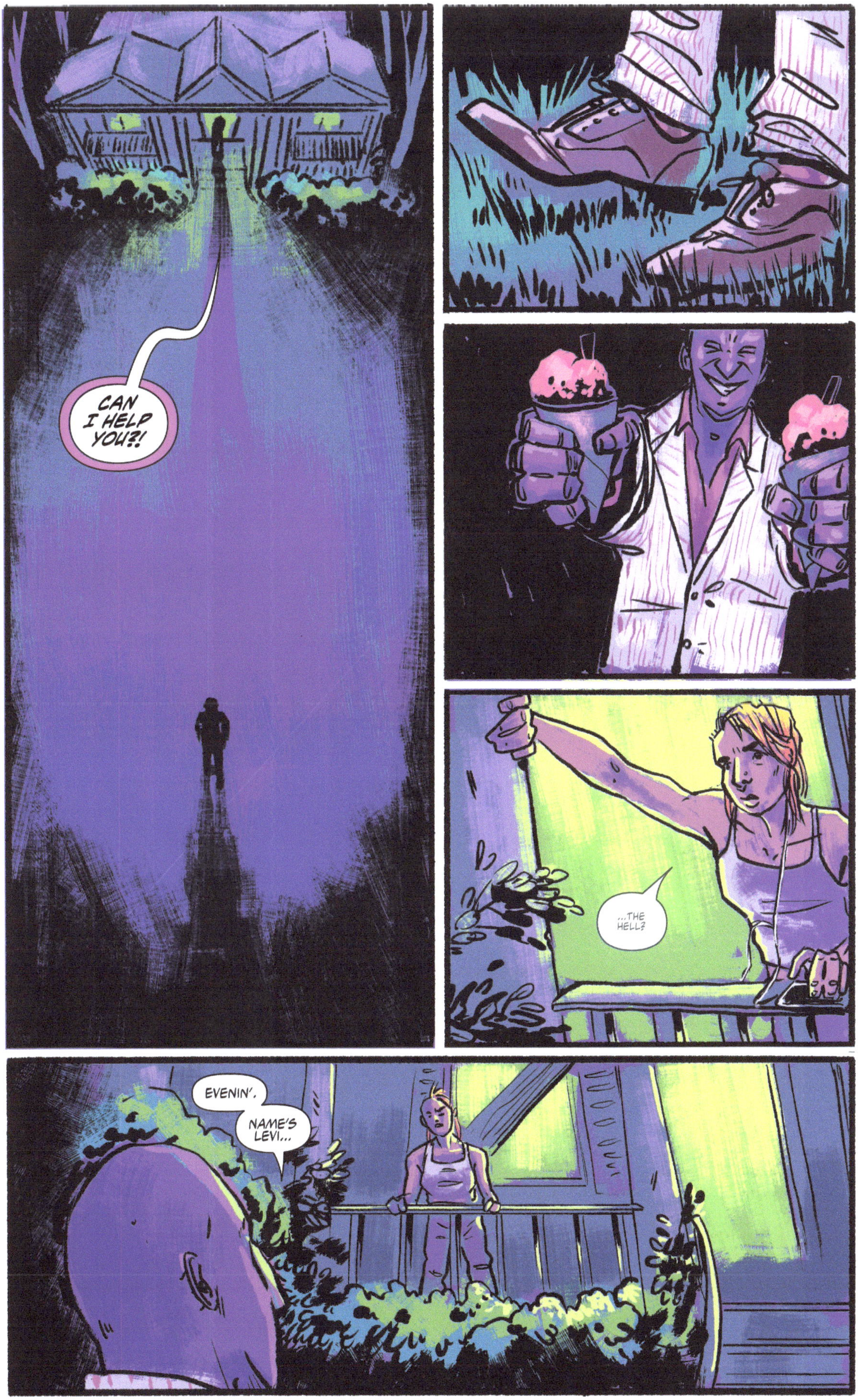

CAN I HELP YOU?!

...LEVI SALEM.
AND I BELIEVE I KNEW YOUR GRANDDAD.
CAN I OFFER YOU A "SNO-BALL?"
IT'S A LOCAL FAVORITE, AS I UNDERSTAND.
TUTTI FRUTTI.

UH, I'M GOOD.
THANKS.

HRMMM...

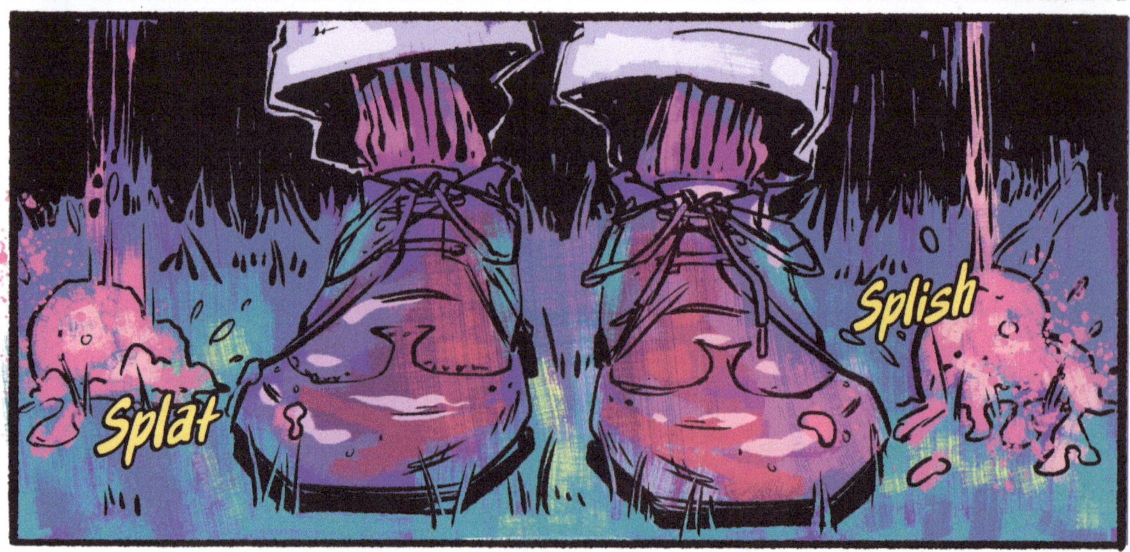
Splat
Splish

IF YOU'RE LOOKING FOR HUDSON, HE'S NOT HERE. HE'S DEAD, ACTUALLY.
YES, OL' HUDSON VAN EVERY. A PRESUMED PASSING, WASN'T IT?
SINCE NO ONE'S SEEN OR HEARD FROM HIM IN SOME TIME?

A SHAME.

YEEAAH, IT'S PRETTY LATE--
THE GUITAR.

"I BELIEVE IT HAS A NAME...
"...DOROTHEA?"

WHAT ABOUT IT?

WELL, YOU SEE...
...AND PERHAPS THIS IS A TOUCH AWKWARD, BUT...
...I LENT IT TO HIM.

BULLSHIT. HE PLAYED THAT THING FOR *DECADES.*
NEVERTHELESS, OUR AGREEMENT--

LOOK, MAN--GO PICK THROUGH SOME OTHER DEAD GUY'S STUFF, OKAY?

EVEN IF THAT GUITAR *WAS* SOMEWHERE AROUND HERE...
...IT'D BE *MINE.* THIS WHOLE PLACE IS.

YOU MEAN TO SAY YOU *DON'T* HAVE IT? THE "DOROTHEA?"

NO ONE'S SEEN IT, DUDE.
IN YEARS. JUST LIKE THEY HAVEN'T SEEN *HIM.*

IT'S ALL IN THE WIKIPEDIA.
SO IF YOU COULD GET THE FUCK OFF MY PROPERTY NOW--?
HRMMM...

SCOFF
GODDAMN CREEP.

THE NEXT DAY.

OKAY, DOROTHÉA...
GUITAR & PIANO

...WHERE THE HELL ARE YOU?

KAFF
KAFF
GROSS, DUDE...

EWW--!
ARE YOU *LEAKING* SOMETHING?!

WHY WOULD SOMEONE, ARGH--!
--EVEN *HAVE* THIS?!

WHOA, WAIT A SECOND...

...
NO GODDAMN WAY.

FWOOSSH
FUCK.
YES.
BONK
PLINK
YIKES.
BINK
PONK

WHAT'S UP WITH YOUR GUTS, LADY?

CLANK
THE HELL...?
SIX...
...SIX...
...SIX?
C'MON --FUCK!

SIGH
WHY THE HELL WOULD YOU LOCK THIS?

JESUS, OLD MAN.
WHAT THE FUCK WERE YOU UP TO?

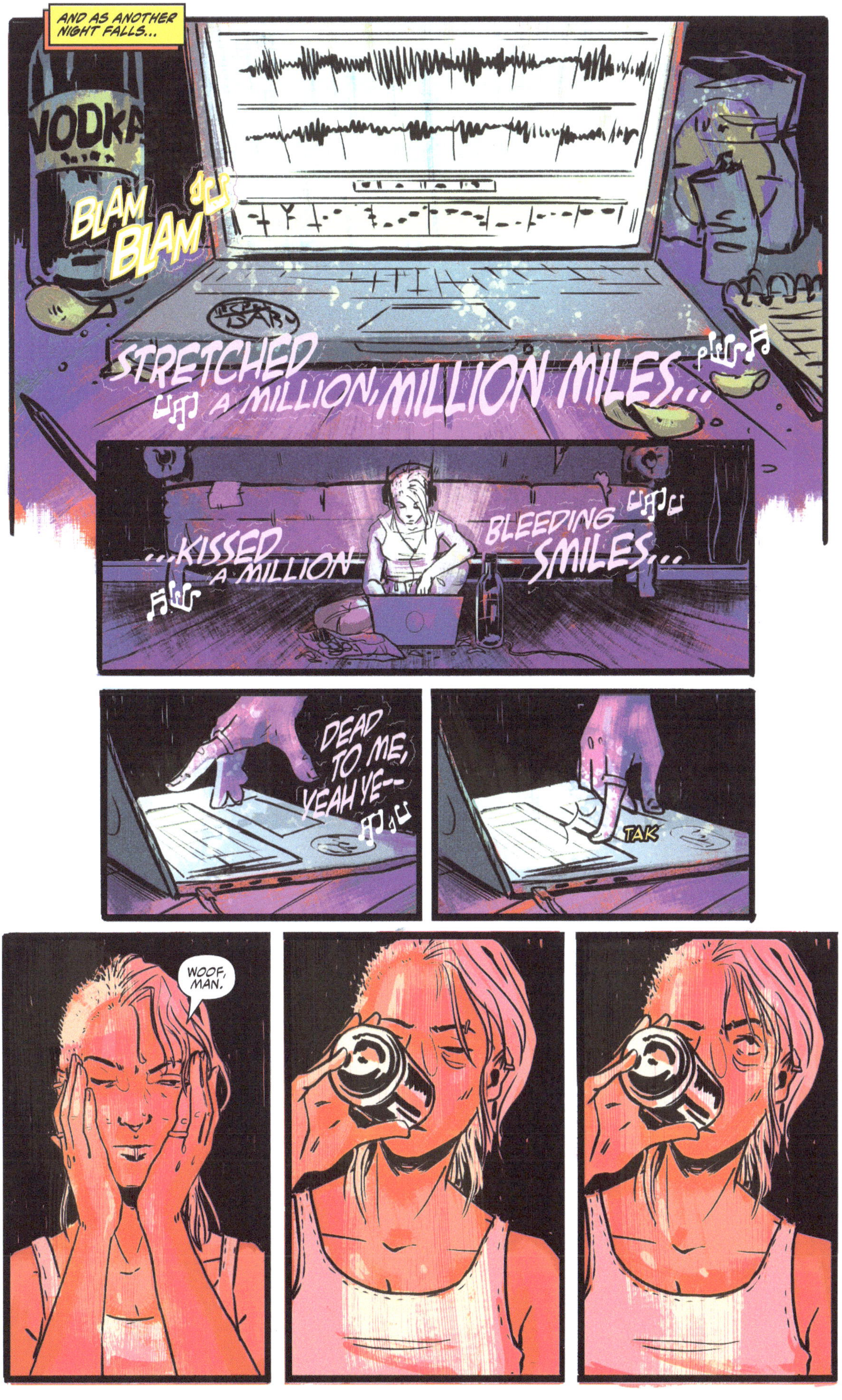

AND AS ANOTHER NIGHT FALLS...

VODKA

BLAM BLAM

STRETCHED A MILLION, MILLION MILES...

...KISSED A MILLION BLEEDING SMILES...

OH.
HIC
HELLO.
MMMM...
LET'S SEE IF I REMEMBER...
AHEM
IT'S LIKE...
MEET ME AT THE GALLOWS...
...AND PLEASE, GIRL, DON'T BE LATE.
SAID, MEET ME AT THE GALLOWS...
...BE THERE HALF PAST EIGHT.
GOTTA APPOINT--
WHUNK

SHIT, WHAT WAS IT?
G7...
...AND A5.
THEN...?
TWANG
GOTTA APPOINTMENT WITH JOHNNY--
BWANK
FUCK!
PWANG
OW!
HEH.

WHUMP
AHH...
HIC
GOTTA APPOINTMENT...
...WITH JOHNNY LAW THERE...
AND SOMETHING...
...SOMETHING...
...SOMETHIIING...

...MMWHAT THE HELL?
SHH-SHH-SHH
JUST A LITTLE MORE...
PERFECT G NOTE
THERE.
GOOD AS NEW.

WHOA--!
WHAT THE SHIT?!
SWICK
GET THE FUCK OUTTA HERE, DUDE!
HRMMM...
I HEARD GUITAR EARLIER AND THOUGHT MAYBE...
THIS IS MY HOUSE, ASSHOLE!
I CAN CUT YOU RIGHT NOW AND THIS BACKWARDS-ASS STATE WOULD PROBABLY GIVE ME A STATUE FOR--

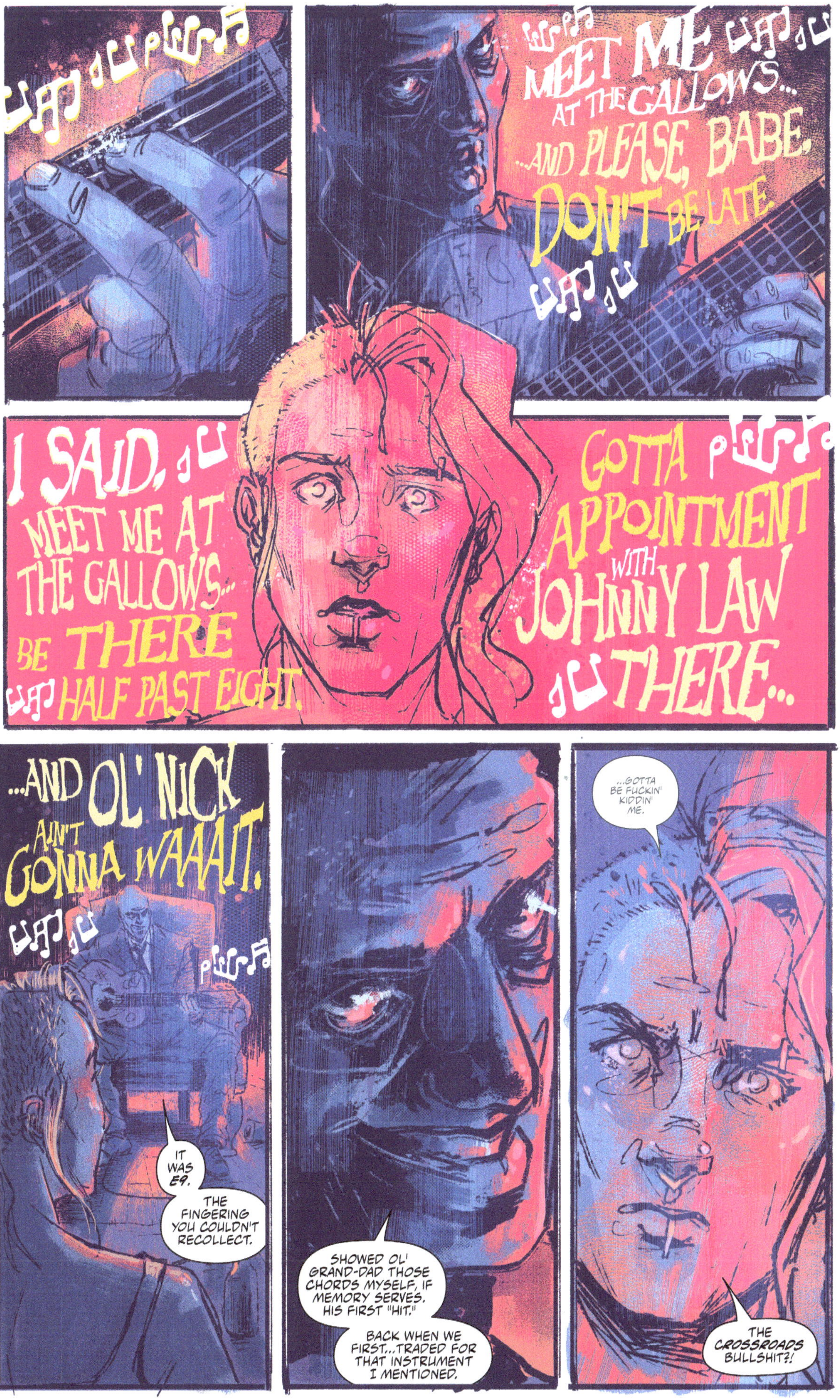

MEET ME AT THE GALLOWS...
...AND PLEASE, BABE, DON'T BE LATE.

I SAID, MEET ME AT THE GALLOWS... BE THERE HALF PAST EIGHT.

GOTTA APPOINTMENT WITH JOHNNY LAW THERE...

IT WAS A FILLING STATION, ACTUALLY.
A FEW MILES OUTSIDE A TOWN CALLED SUGAR LAND.
:KAFF:
"TEXAS" THEY USED TO CALL IT.
WHAT THEY CALL IT NOW, I WOULD NOT KNOW.
LOOK DICKWIPE, I'VE BEEN HEARING THIS SAME CRAP SINCE I WAS IN KINDERGARTEN.
"GRANDPA 'SOLD HIS SOUL' FOR A GUITAR FROM HELL...
"...SO EVERY SONG HE'D PLAY WOULD SOUND PERFECT?
"THAT'S WHY YOU'RE STALKING ME RIGHT NOW?!"
IT WAS A HIPPIE FUCKING GHOST STORY, MAN.
IT WAS MARKETING.

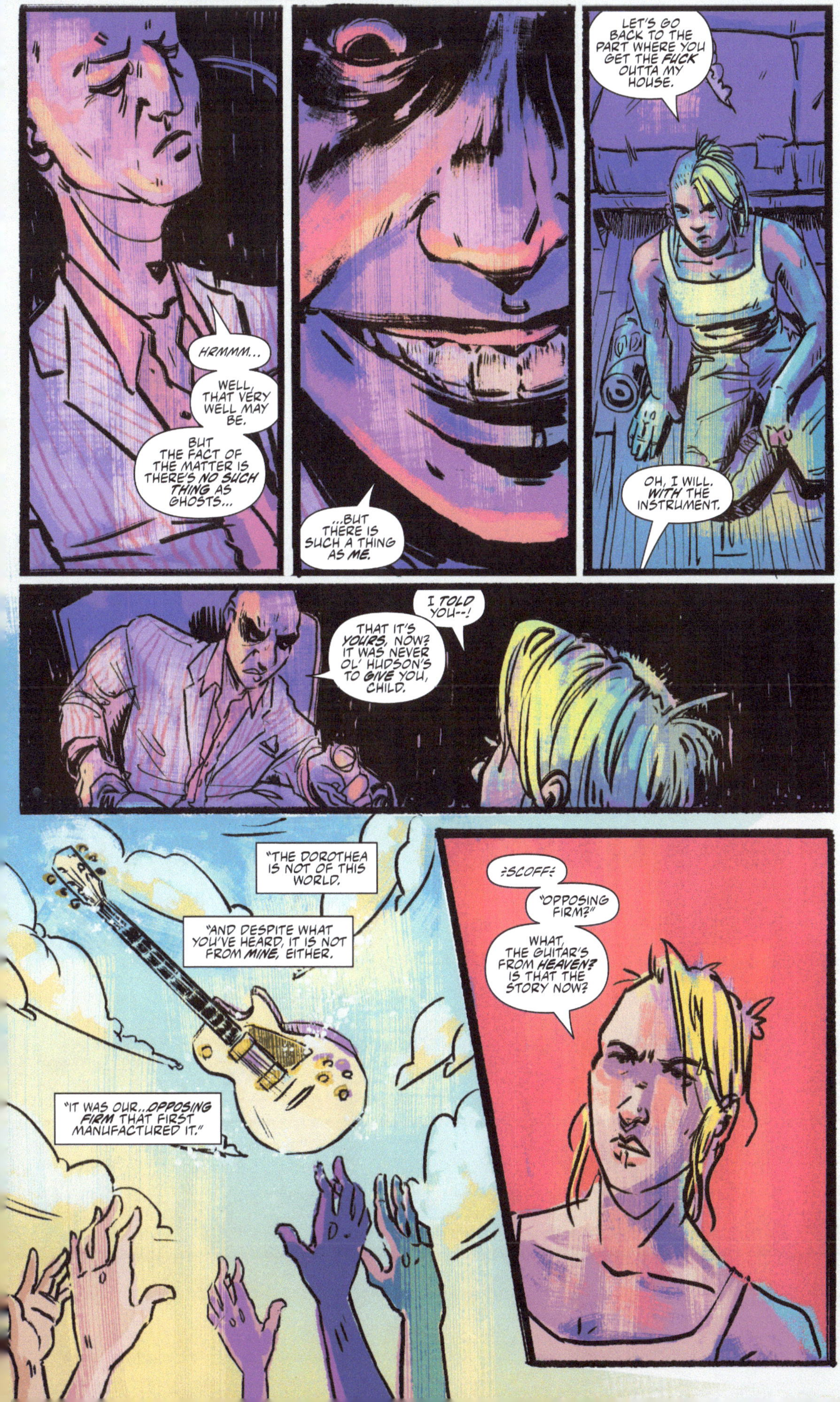

I TOLD YOU--!

THAT IT'S YOURS, NOW? IT WAS NEVER OL' HUDSON'S TO GIVE YOU, CHILD.

"THE DOROTHEA IS NOT OF THIS WORLD.

"AND DESPITE WHAT YOU'VE HEARD, IT IS NOT FROM MINE, EITHER.

"IT WAS OUR...OPPOSING FIRM THAT FIRST MANUFACTURED IT."

≈SCOFF≈

"OPPOSING FIRM?"

WHAT, THE GUITAR'S FROM HEAVEN? IS THAT THE STORY NOW?

I WAS NOT PRIVY TO THE DETAILS OF ITS *ACQUISITION.*
I WAS, HOWEVER, CHARGED WITH ITS *DISTRIBUTION.*

SEE, AT *MY* FIRM, PERSUASION IS OUR PRODUCT.
AND WHILE YOU CAN'T PUT FAME AND *FORTUNE* IN THE MAMMALIAN HAND...

...YOU *CAN* PUT AN INSTRUMENT.
SOMETHING IT CAN SEE, CAN *TOUCH.*
AND, WELL... THAT CAN DO A WHOLE LOT OF THE PERSUADING *FOR* YOU.

DOES IT MATTER WHERE A THING LIKE THAT IS *FROM?*
MY PROFESSIONAL OPINION? NO, NOT REALLY.

ALL THAT MATTERS IS...
...THAT IT *SHINES.*

KSSH
SHIT!
HOW'D YOU...?
DO THAT AGAIN.
NO, THANK YOU.
JESUS, DUDE--IF YOU'RE TRYING TO FREAK ME OUT...
...A-FUCKING-PLUS, OKAY?!
BUT THE GUITAR IS SERIOUSLY NOT HERE.
WHEREVER HUDSON WENT, HE PROBABLY TOOK IT WITH HIM!

MM. UNLIKELY.
THE MUSK OF MY COMPETITION IS ALL OVER THESE WOODS.
THEY SENSE IT, TOO. THE DOROTHEA. IT'S CLOSE.

"AND LET ME TELL YOU, THESE COMPETITORS OF MINE?
"THEY ARE A FAR CRY FROM THESE CHERUBIC OVERSEERS YOU IMAGINE."

NO, NO, CHILD--THEY ARE ABOMINATIONS. VICIOUS ONES.
ONE HUNDRED PERCENT VILE. HONEST AND TRULY.
ALL THE MORE REASON TO SQUARE THIS BUSINESS TONIGHT. WITH ME.

AND AVOID ANY UNPLEASANT ENCOUNTERS.

BUT WHAT IF...
...WHAT IF THEY'D LET ME KEEP IT, THOUGH?
YOU.
WITH THE INSTRUMENT.
THAT'S... NOT HOW IT WORKS.
WHY NOT?
MY GRANDPA SOLD MILLIONS OF RECORDS...
...PERFORMED ALL OVER THE WORLD.
"HE ACTUALLY, LIKE, MEANT SOMETHING TO PEOPLE WITH THAT GUITAR.
"I BET HEAVEN LOVED THAT SHIT."
YOU DON'T THINK I COULD DO THE SAME THING?

"MOTHERFUCKER, I ALREADY DO.
"I GOT A MILLION FOLLOWERS ON THREE DIFFERENT PLATFORMS...
"...TWO VIRAL SONGS OFF AN INDIE RECORD I PRODUCED...
"...AND YOUR MOM'S FAVORITE CHECKOUT LINE TABLOID HANGING ON MY EVERY GODDAMN WORD."
LEGAL SHIT ASIDE...
...FUCK SOME NORMIE GETTING THE GUITAR NEXT.
IT SHOULD BE ME.
LIKE, OBVIOUSLY.
SO, YOU'RE THE CRÈME DE LA CRÈME, HUH?
WELL, ALLOW ME TO ENLIGHTEN YOU.
"FROM A QUALITY STANDPOINT, YOUR KIND ALL COME FROM THE SAME, TRIED 'N' TRUE RECIPE.
"EVERY LAST ONE OF YOU, FROM THE VERY BEGINNING.
"SO, THE IDEA THAT ANY ONE OF YOU IS BETTER, MORE DESERVING THAN THE OTHER?
"I MEAN, THAT WAS ONE OF OUR FIRM'S FIRST PRODUCTS!
"CHILD, THAT IS OUR BREAD AND BUTTER."

"THERE'S ONLY ONE WRINKLE THAT MAKES ANY OF YOU STAND OUT--DESPERATION.
'OL' GRANDDAD, HE HAD IT IN SPADES. HE NEEDED TO TRADE.
"IN HIS BONES."

BUT YOU? WHAT HAVE YOU EVER NEEDED?
YOU EXPECT THE DOROTHEA TO BE HANDED TO YOU?

WHY?

BECAUSE EVERYTHING ELSE IN YOUR LITTLE, SILLY LIFE WAS, TOO?
FUCK YOU, DUDE...

AHEM
THERE BETTER BE A GUITAR IN THAT SATCHEL.
SHIT, I THOUGHT I HAD A LIGHT IN HERE.

WANNA HIT ME?

HRMMM...

VERY WELL.

KATSSH
BLAM
BA BLAM
BAM
BLAM
BLAM
AND HERE'S--
--FOR CALLIN' ME--

BAFF
--CHILD!
...THE FUCK?
CHIT CHIT CHIT
CHIT
CHIT CHIT
CHIT CHIT
CHIT
BZZOARR
CHIT CHIT
WHAT THE SHIT?!
CHIT CHIT
CHIT CHIT
CHIT CHIT

ARRGH--
FUCK!
CHIT CHIT CHIT
CHIT CHIT
CHIT CHIT
CHIT CHIT
THUNK
GAH!
UGH!
MEET ME
AT THE GALLOWS...

...AND PLEASE, BABE, DON'T BE LATE.

FUCKIN' SONG.
FUCKING "E9."
HOW THE FUCK DID HE--

I SAID, MEET ME AT THE GALLOWS... BE THERE HALF PAST EIGHT.

G7, A5, E9...
...SEVEN, FIVE, NINE...
...SEVEN, FIVE, NI--

KLACK
YES!

SQUEEEE

...
MOTHERFUCKER.
IF THEY MAKE ME--
=KAFF=
GO TO THERAPY 'CAUSE OF THIS--
=HRRK=
I SWEAR TO FUCKIN' GOD, DUDE...

BRING YOUR HANDS TOGETHER NOW!

GROSS.
GROSS.
GROSS.

VZZT VZZT

KRAK
KRAAACKLE

GOTTA APPOINTMENT WITH JOHNNY LAW THERE...

AND OL' NICK...
...AIN'T GONNA WAIT.

SKEE--ÖWW!

KA-
BOOOM

...NNG?

GOTCHU.

THOOM

THOOM

THOOM

THOOM

NO-- WAIT!
I NEED IT.
P-PLEASE.
NO!!
NO...

WHUMP

-KAFF KAFF-
NOW YOU'VE GOT IT...

...GOT THAT WRINKLE.

YOU'D TRADE NOW, WOULDN'T YOU? FOR THE INSTRUMENT?
AIN'T THAT A SHAME--
--I'M FRESH OUT!
A-- AHAH-

AH-- AHAH-- HA-- HAHA! HA! HA!
THE END.

CREATOR BIO

ROB PILKINGTON

IS A WRITER BASED IN LOS ANGELES. HE'S THE CO-CREATOR OF *DAME FROM THE DARK* FROM TKO STUDIOS, WAS NAMED A RUNNER-UP IN TOP COW'S 2020 TALENT HUNT, AND HAS WRITTEN SHORT COMICS FOR VARIOUS SMALL PRESS AND INDIE ANTHOLOGIES.

HEATHER VAUGHAN

IS AN AWARD-WINNING, PHILADELPHIA-BASED ILLUSTRATOR WHOSE CLIENTS INCLUDE MARVEL, IDW, WALT DISNEY TELEVISION, 20TH TELEVISION, AND THE PHILADELPHIA EAGLES, AMONG OTHERS. SHE'S THE RECIPIENT OF AWARDS AND HONORS FROM AMERICAN ILLUSTRATION, 3X3 MAGAZINE, COMMUNICATION ARTS, AND SOCIETY OF ILLUSTRATORS LOS ANGELES.

JEROME GAGNON

IS A RINGO AWARD NOMINATED COMIC BOOK LETTERER AND GRAPHIC DESIGNER FROM MONTREAL WITH WORK ON SUCH TITLES AS *GRANITE STATE PUNK*, *COINS OF JUDAS*, AND *HOLIDAY SPIRITS*.

ERIN KEEPERS

IS A COMIC BOOK WRITER AND EDITOR WITH A MASTER'S IN COMIC BOOK STUDIES AND A PASSION FOR CRITICAL STORY ANALYSIS. LATELY, MANY OF HER COMICS HAVE BEEN ABOUT RESISTANCE IN THE FACE OF INJUSTICE. FOR NO REASON WHATSOEVER. RECENT CREDITS INCLUDE THE MEDIEVAL SATIRE COMIC *NOBODY'S PRINCESS*, AS WELL AS A VARIETY OF ANTHOLOGY PIECES AND EDUCATIONAL COMICS.

MARCUS MCNEAL

IS AN AWARD-NOMINATED EDITOR AND PUBLISHER BASED IN SOUTHERN CALIFORNIA. AS FOUNDER AND CEO OF ODYSSEY COMICS, HE HAS DEVELOPED CHARACTER-DRIVEN TITLES WITH CREATIVE TEAMS AROUND THE WORLD INCLUDING *TWILIGHT CUSTARD*, *IVERRIAN: CURSE OF THE CROWN*, AND *CRITICAL MASS*.

AN UNRESOLVED CHORD

BY MARCUS MCNEAL

As a publisher, it's a rare occasion to receive a comic pitch that is an instant "YES", but *Slight Return* was such a project. Having previously collaborated with Rob on our science fiction anthology *Critical Mass*, I knew he was a writer with an uncanny sense of storytelling and had the kind of creative vision that perfectly aligns with Odyssey. So when he handed me his deck with stunning pages by Heather and dynamic letters from Jerome, I knew instantly this was a story I wanted to help deliver to readers.

To help make this a reality, I tapped my dear friend and #1 at Odyssey Comics, Erin Keepers, to bring her unique editorial pedigree to this project. With that, the result was never in doubt. What wasn't expected was how much this book would become representative of so much for us, both professionally and personally.

Firstly, I believe *Slight Return* distills our entire ethos as a studio—a project where the incredible collaborative spirit drives everyone to deliver their best. This is the kind of story we want to tell, crafted in the way we want to make comics, and done so with a level of creative talent that left nothing to be desired. Perhaps more so than any book we have published before, *Slight Return* feels like the kind of project we were destined to make. If you love this book, and we hope you do, expect more things like it in the very near future.

Secondly, as I read Rob's first draft something resonated deeply with me. Our protagonist Theo Van Every, and her entire struggle, is in search of one thing; grace. Not just in the form of a divine guitar, but grace from her failings, and grace from the worst of her own inclinations. In a period where the world has often made creative pursuits difficult, exhausting, and fraught with missteps, so many of us are looking for grace. We're looking for the permission and power to continue, or in some cases, begin again. The question *Slight Return* poses to Theo, and to all of us, is whether or not we pursue grace in earnest, whether it's in conviction or commodity.

The answer to that helped us see what's worth holding on to in the end.

That's where real legacy is created. Not the kind that is handed down like some derelict property, but the kind clawed from the mud and driven by passion. *Slight Return* isn't just another entry in our library—it's a statement piece. It represents Odyssey's commitment to storytelling that's unafraid to take its time. To feel something. To be vulnerable, strange, and personal.

We're proud to bring this story into the world. Not because it's flashy, but because it lingers.

Like a chord still echoing in the air. 

MEET ME AT THE GALLOWS...

www.ingramcontent.com/pod-product-compliance
Lightning Source LLC
LaVergne TN
LVHW070210110826
845147LV00002B/557

* 9 7 9 8 9 9 5 2 4 7 4 1 8 *